Lian tightened the helmet strap around the chin, and when he stepped back in, he took a *hard* practice swing—harder than Harlan remembered him ever taking before.

And when the first pitch came, he took a powerful swing . . .

And missed!

That was something he almost never did. Harlan had only seen him strike out a couple of times all year.

Gerstein laughed, and so did Schulman. "He wants to knock one out of here," Schulman yelled.

Lian motioned with his left arm as if to say, "Just throw it, and watch what I can do."

The next pitch was a firecracker of a fastball, and Lian swung so hard his feet left the ground.

But he *connected*.

*Look for these books about the
Angel Park All-Stars*

PLAY-OFF

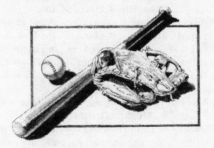

By Dean Hughes

Illustrated by Dennis Lyall

Bullseye Books • Alfred A. Knopf
New York

A BULLSEYE BOOK PUBLISHED BY ALFRED A. KNOPF, INC.
Copyright © 1991 by Dean Hughes
Cover art copyright © 1991 by Rick Ormond
Interior illustrations copyright © 1991 by Dennis Lyall
ANGEL PARK ALL-STARS characters copyright © 1989
by Alfred A. Knopf, Inc.

Library of Congress Cataloging-in-Publication Data
Hughes, Dean, 1943–
Play-off / by Dean Hughes ; illustrated by Dennis Lyall.
p.   cm.—(Angel Park all-stars ; 13)
Summary: Because Lian Jie is so small, no one on the Dodgers
takes him seriously, until they realize he's a baseball expert.
ISBN 0-679-81540-6 (pbk.)—ISBN 0-679-91540-0 (lib. bdg.)
[1. Baseball—Fiction.] I. Lyall, Dennis, ill. II. Title.
III. Series: Hughes, Dean, 1943– Angel Park all-stars ; 13.
PZ7.H87312P1   1991
[Fic]—dc20   90-49765

RL: 4.5
First Bullseye Books edition: July 1991
Manufactured in the United States of America
10 9 8 7 6 5 4 3 2 1

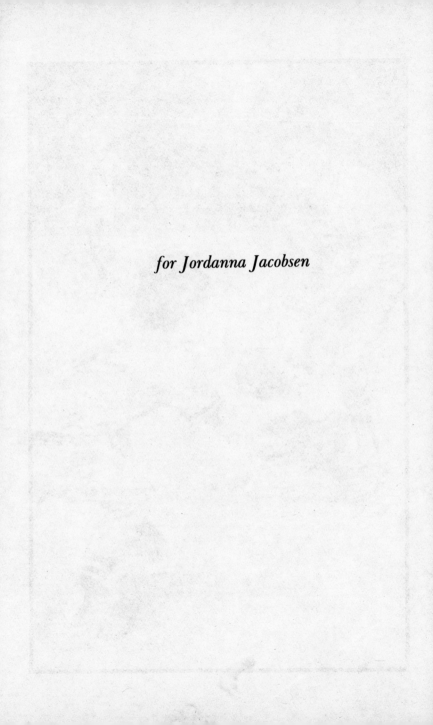

for Jordanna Jacobsen

★1★

Hard-Hit Grounder

The Angel Park Dodgers needed only three outs to finish off the San Lorenzo Mariners.

The Mariners had scored first, but the Dodgers had come back and tied the score in the third inning and then gone ahead in the fourth. They were now ahead 9 to 5 in the last inning.

Harlan Sloan wasn't really worried. Eddie Boschi had pitched the first two innings for the Dodgers, and he had given up all five runs. Since Jonathan "Swat" Swingle had taken over on the mound, the Mariners hadn't even had a hit.

Harlan was playing catcher, and his hand was stinging. Jonathan was really *burning* the pitches in.

The first batter in the sixth inning was Klein, the shortstop who batted ninth.

Jonathan popped a couple of fastballs, and the kid swung wildly—and late. Harlan doubted he even *saw* the ball.

But then Swat tried his slow curve, and Klein sort of stuck his bat out and blooped the ball toward Kenny Sandoval at short. Kenny charged the ball and took it on a short hop.

It was a great pickup. He came up smoothly, cocked his arm, and fired the ball to . . .

No!

The ball slipped out of his hand!

It flipped away and rolled across the grass.

By the time Kenny picked it up, the runner had already crossed first base.

Kenny shook his head and pounded his glove, and then he said, "Sorry," to Jonathan, and tossed the ball to him.

"That's okay," Jonathan said.

Everyone knew that Kenny was a great infielder. But even the best could make an error once in a while.

Besides, the Dodgers still had that big lead.

The top of the order was coming up—some good hitters. But Jonathan hadn't had any trouble with them the last time around.

Jonathan really went to work on Cisco, the left fielder. He threw nothing but flames. But Cisco kept fouling off Jonathan's good pitches and taking the ones out of the strike zone. He finally worked the count to 3 and 2.

And then Jonathan threw a fastball that almost blew Harlan's mitt away.

Strike three!

Or that's what Harlan thought. But when he stood up and yelled, "Way to go! One down," he heard the umpire behind him say, "That's ball four. Take your base."

Harlan spun around. "What?"

"The ball was low," the umpire said.

Harlan didn't believe it, but he didn't argue. That was a rule with Coach Wilkens: players weren't allowed to argue with the umpire.

Besides, deep down Harlan still wasn't worried. He crouched behind the plate again, and he told himself that Jonathan would still get these guys.

And he did.

Or at least he got two of them. He struck out the next two batters, making them look bad. Now the Dodgers were in good shape.

But Rodriguez, the cleanup batter, wasn't so sure the game was over. He met one of Jonathan's wicked fastballs and drove it all the way to the fence in left field. Two runs scored, and suddenly that four-run lead was cut in half.

Jonathan kicked the pitching rubber. Harlan knew he was mainly mad that he had given up the runs. He wasn't really worried about losing.

All the same, the situation was getting a little tight. The Dodgers had already lost one game in the second half of the season. A loss to the Mariners—one of the weaker teams in the league—would blow their chances for the championship.

Just as Jonathan was getting ready to take his sign from Harlan, Lian Jie, the Dodgers' second baseman, yelled, "Time out!" and trotted to the mound. Harlan wondered what was up, so he ran out to see.

Lian was from Taiwan, but he had been

in the United States for a year now, and his English was pretty good. "I watched this batter last week," Lian told Jonathan. "He can't hit curve balls. Throw him curve balls."

"Hey, he's a rookie. He can't hit *anything* I pitch."

"He's a pretty good hitter," Lian said. "But curve balls scare him. He jumps back."

Jonathan laughed. "Okay, Lian. I'll throw him curve balls."

But Harlan knew that Jonathan hadn't taken Lian seriously. Hardly anyone did. Lian was so small that most people thought he ought to be in T-ball instead of Little League. Even the Dodgers teased him a lot about his size.

But Lian knew the game.

Harlan ran back to his position, and he called for a curve. Jonathan threw a good one, and Watson, the batter, bailed out just the way Lian said he would. The ball broke over the plate for a strike.

Second pitch, same thing. Now they were only one strike away from their win.

But Harlan knew they better not come with the same pitch three times in a row.

He signaled for a fastball and then set up his target outside. He wanted Jonathan to waste one, and see if they could get Watson to go after it. If he didn't, they could come back to the curve.

But Jonathan didn't go outside. He blasted his fastball right over the plate.

And Watson socked it back up the middle for a single.

Rodriguez scored, and suddenly the lead was down to one.

That was bad enough.

But then Harlan made a mistake.

Jonathan was angry now. He let Korman, the catcher, get set. Then he let loose a wild fastball. But the ball bounced in the dirt, wide of the plate. Harlan tried to reach for the ball and didn't get over with his body to block the pitch.

The ball bounced off his glove, and the runner moved to second.

Michael Wilkens, the assistant coach, yelled, "You have to block those, Harlan," but Harlan knew that already. Why hadn't he done it?

Now the tying run was in scoring position.

Harlan *was* worried now.

Korman had good bat control. He was hard to strike out.

Harlan flashed a curve ball signal to Jonathan. At the same time he noticed that Lian took a couple of quick steps to his right.

Korman wasn't fooled by the curve. He held his ground and jabbed the ball hard. The ball scooted past the mound and on up the middle. Harlan was sure the tying run would . . .

But Lian dashed to his right, and at the last moment he stretched all out and snagged the ball. He had stopped the run from scoring. Still, he was too far off balance to turn and throw.

But Kenny had been charging toward the ball too, and Lian—still off balance—flipped the ball with his glove hand. Kenny took the relay as though the two players had been going for a double play.

And Kenny made a perfect throw to first.

And *got* the runner!

The game was over.

The play was *amazing!*

Most guys never would have gotten to the ball, and even then they wouldn't have thought to toss it to the shortstop for the throw to first.

All the Dodgers mobbed Lian. Harlan charged out toward them, whooping and leaping in the air.

Jonathan was jumping around too. "You saved the game!" he yelled to Lian. "Way to go!"

He grabbed Lian and tried to hoist him up on his shoulders. But Lian didn't like that. He pulled back.

Jonathan laughed instead and said, "Lian, you're a little star!" And then he reached out and patted Lian on the head.

Harlan saw Lian's smile disappear. He turned, suddenly, and walked away.

Harlan thought he knew why.

"Hey, Lian," Harlan said, and he pronounced the name correctly. "Lee-en." Some of the boys, especially Jonathan, called him "Leon," but Harlan knew that Lian didn't really like that.

Lian looked around.

"How did you know that kid was going to hit the ball up the middle?" Harlan asked. "I saw you move over. If you hadn't done that, you never would have gotten to the ball."

"I saw you signal for a curve," Lian said. "On a fastball he would swing late, but not on a curve."

Harlan looked over at his friend Kenny. "That makes sense. Do you ever do that, Kenny?"

"No. I shift over for left-handers, but I never even thought of shifting for different pitches."

"My coach in Taiwan taught me," Lian said.

"You must have had good coaches over there," Jacob said.

"Very good coaches. Coach Wilkens is a very good coach too." Lian hesitated for a second or two, and then he added, "But in Taiwan, all the players help each other. No one makes someone . . . feel bad."

Now Harlan knew for sure. "I don't think Jonathan meant to make you feel bad when he said you were little. He just—"

"I *am* little," Lian said. "But I'm not a baby dog, to pat on the head."

"Don't worry about Jonathan," Kenny said.

"You're probably the best all-around player on our team, and we all know that."

But Lian still looked unhappy. He walked over and got his bike and left.

Harlan wondered what he could do.

BOX SCORE, GAME 16

San Lorenzo Mariners 8

	ab	r	h	rbi
Cisco lf	2	3	1	0
Smagler 2b	2	1	0	0
Cast cf	3	1	0	0
Rodriguez 1b	4	2	2	5
Watson p	2	0	1	1
Korman c	3	0	0	0
Sullivan 3b	3	0	1	2
Ford rf	1	0	0	0
Klein ss	2	1	0	0
Bernhardt 2b	2	0	0	0
Casper cf	1	0	0	0
Rondeau rf	1	0	0	0
ttl	**26**	**8**	**5**	**8**

Angel Park Dodgers 9

	ab	r	h	rbi
Jie 2b	2	1	1	0
White 3b	4	0	2	1
Sandoval ss	3	1	2	1
Swingle lf, p	3	2	2	2
Malone cf	2	1	1	2
Roper 1b	2	1	1	1
Boschi p	2	0	0	0
Bacon c	2	0	0	0
Scott rf	3	1	2	2
Sloan c	0	1	0	0
Riddle cf	0	1	0	0
Ruiz lf	1	0	0	0
	24	**9**	**11**	**9**

Mariners 4 1 0 0 0 3—8
Dodgers 3 0 2 1 3 x—9

★ 2 ★

"Must" Game

The Dodgers had now won 5 and lost 1 in the second half of the season. The only trouble was, the Giants and the Reds both kept winning too. The three teams were tied for first.

The Giants had won the first-half championship. The Dodgers had to come in first in the second half to have a chance at winning the season championship.

On Saturday the Dodgers would be playing the Reds, so that would be a "must" game.

And when Saturday came, the Dodgers were ready. The Reds' players had the biggest mouths in the league, but Coach

Wilkens told his players how to deal with that: "Nothing will shut them up faster than lots of runs, good pitching, good defense. Just don't start jawing back and forth with them."

Harlan knew that was true. But when Lian walked out to lead off the first inning, the Reds started all the razzing stuff, right from the beginning.

"Hey, Dodgers, is that your mascot?" one of the Reds yelled from the outfield. "What is he, an elf?"

And the shortstop shouted, "Hey, kid, you can stand on a box if you want. I know it's hard for you to see over the plate."

Billy Bacon yelled back at him, "Hey, you're going to need a plate in your *skull* after he drives a shot off your forehead."

Coach Wilkens walked over to the dugout and said, "Billy, what did I just tell you? Let's stay out of this."

But that was easier said than done. Even Lian's clean single into left field didn't shut them up.

When Lian stopped at first, Harlan heard the tall first baseman say, "Hey, that was a nice hit—for a midget."

All the Reds' infielders laughed. But Jimmy Gerstein, the Reds' smart-mouthed pitcher, pointed at Lian and said, "That's the last hit you get off me today. I wasn't warmed up."

The truth was, he looked plenty warm against Henry White and against Kenny. Neither one hit the ball hard. But Lian played it smart on the bases and moved up on each ground ball. So with two out, he was on third.

When Gerstein tossed his first pitch to Jonathan, Lian suddenly broke for the plate. He threw on the brakes just as quickly and dared the catcher to throw.

Schulman, the catcher, didn't go for it. He held onto the ball and ran up the line. Lian had to go back to third.

Still, he had Gerstein watching now. And maybe that's why he grooved a pitch to Jonathan. Jonathan whacked the ball *out of sight* for a home run, and the Dodgers were on top 2 to 0.

It was a good start, and it did quiet down the Reds.

But the Dodgers couldn't seem to get much going after that. Gerstein settled down and got the last out, and he mowed them down easily in the second and third.

In the fourth, the Dodgers loaded the bases, partly because of another hit by Lian, but they couldn't bring anyone home.

All the same, Kenny was pitching great, and at the end of four innings, the Dodgers' two-run lead was holding up.

And then in the top of the fifth the Dodgers exploded. Kenny opened the inning with a triple off the fence in left. Jonathan drove him in with a smash double. Sterling Malone and Jenny Roper followed with singles, and the Dodgers had two runs in and two on.

And no one out!

It looked as if the Dodgers might run away with the game. That's when Ben Riddle entered the game in Jacob Scott's spot. He had some good cuts, but Gerstein bore down and struck him out.

One out.

Billy substituted for Harlan and rolled a grounder to the left side. The rally seemed to be dying.

But the shortstop tried to hurry his throw and pulled the first baseman off the bag.

Things were suddenly better than ever.

The bases were loaded and the Dodgers had a chance to blow the game wide open.

Anthony Ruiz was coming up. And he was not an easy out the way he had been early in the season.

But this time Gerstein was too much for him. Anthony popped up to the infield.

Two outs. Bases still loaded. Top of the order coming up.

And that meant Lian.

Harlan could see that Gerstein meant business. He was already mad that someone as little as Lian had gotten two hits off him.

Schulman started in on Lian immediately. "Hey, little guy. Don't even *think* about getting another hit today."

Lian paid no attention. He took his stance and concentrated on the pitcher.

But Gerstein wasn't winding up. He yelled, "I'll knock your head off—if I can throw the ball that *low*."

Gerstein got a good chewing out from the umpire. But he didn't seem to care. And Lian didn't seem bothered either. He took a couple of practice swings, and then he set himself.

Jonathan's voice boomed from the dugout. "Hey, Gerstein, look out. Our little man is going to break your *ankles* with one of his line drives."

Lian suddenly threw up his hand to call time-out, and he stepped out of the box.

Harlan saw Lian take a hard look at Jonathan. He knew what Lian must be thinking. It was one thing to take that stuff from the Reds, but he didn't need it from his own team.

Lian tightened the helmet strap around the chin, and when he stepped back in, he took a *hard* practice swing—harder than Harlan remembered him ever taking before.

And when the first pitch came, he took a powerful swing . . .

And missed!

That was something he almost never did. Harlan had only seen him strike out a couple of times all year.

Gerstein laughed, and so did Schulman. "He wants to knock one out of here," Schulman yelled.

Lian motioned with his left arm as if to

say, "Just throw it, and watch what I can do."

The next pitch was a firecracker of a fast-ball, and Lian swung so hard his feet left the ground.

But he *connected.*

And he hit a long fly. Harrison, the center fielder, had to run hard to get back to it. But he turned around and made the catch.

Gerstein walked off, rather relieved, and he and Schulman didn't have a whole lot to say. They had seen that Lian could hit the ball a long way when he wanted to.

But Harlan saw something that surprised him more than the hard swing Lian had taken. Lian slammed the bat on the ground and then kicked it.

Harlan ran Lian's glove out to him, and he said, "Lian, you really *smacked* that ball."

"One time I will hit a home run," Lian said. "Then no one will laugh at me again." He turned and ran out to second base.

Harlan was worried.

So was Coach Wilkens—although he hadn't heard what Lian had said. "Lian," he called, "a single would have scored some runs. Don't start swinging for the fences."

Lian didn't respond, but the Reds' bench did. They all picked up on the coach's words. "Hey, little boy. Don't try to be a home-run hitter. You're not big enough."

Lian didn't look at them. He didn't show any emotion. But when the first batter hit a ball in the hole to his left, he went after it like a wildcat. He got to the ball quickly, fielded it, spun, and made a perfect throw.

Jenny yelled, "Nice play, Lian."

And Lian pumped his arm as if to say, "You bet it was." He gave the Reds a long look, and Harlan knew what he was saying: "If you think I'm so little, then what do you think of that?"

No one was saying much of anything in the Reds' dugout. They were quickly going down to defeat. Kenny finished them off without giving up a run. It wasn't often that the Reds got shut out, and they definitely didn't like it.

But the Dodgers didn't have to give them a hard time. All they had to do was slap hands with the players and say, "Good game," maybe with a grin on their faces.

The Reds could hardly stand that.

The Dodgers thought it was great fun.

And they enjoyed the praise they got from their coach. Afterward, Harlan walked home with his fourth-grade friends, Kenny and Jacob Scott.

As they walked down the street almost everyone they saw wanted to know how the game had gone. And the people were happy when they heard the Dodgers had beaten the Reds. The whole town of Angel Park was proud of its Little League team.

But Harlan had something on his mind. "I'm sort of worried about Lian," Harlan told his friends.

"Why? He had a great game," Jacob said.

"I know, but I'm pretty sure he was trying to hit a home run that last time up."

"Yeah, well, he almost did it," Jacob said.

But Kenny knew what Harlan was talking about. "He shouldn't go for homers," he told Jacob. "He's a lead-off batter, and he's great at poking those little line drives that get him on base."

"Sure," Jacob said, "but who wants to hit lame little hits all the time? I don't blame him for wanting to go downtown with one once in a while."

Kenny smiled and said, "Yeah, I know. But my dad always says you have to know what *you* can do. Lian's just not a home-run hitter."

That made sense to Harlan. But he wasn't sure it made sense to Lian anymore.

BOX SCORE, GAME 17

Angel Park Dodgers 4

	ab	r	h	rbi
Jie 2b	4	1	2	0
White 3b	4	0	1	0
Sandoval p	4	1	2	0
Swingle ss	4	2	2	3
Malone cf	4	0	2	1
Roper 1b	3	0	2	0
Scott rf	2	0	0	0
Sloan c	1	0	1	0
Boschi lf	2	0	0	0
Riddle rf	1	0	0	0
Bacon c	1	0	0	0
Ruiz 1b	1	0	0	0
ttl	**31**	**4**	**12**	**4**

Cactus Hills Reds 0

	ab	r	h	rbi
Trulis 2b	3	0	1	0
Schulman c	3	0	1	0
Gerstein p	3	0	1	0
Higdon ss	3	0	1	0
Rutter 3b	2	0	1	0
Young lf	1	0	0	0
Charles 1b	2	0	0	0
Lum rf	1	0	0	0
Harrison cf	2	0	0	0
Hileman rf	1	0	0	0
Alfini lf	1	0	0	0
Bonthuis cf	1	0	0	0
	23	**0**	**5**	**0**

Dodgers	2 0 0	0 2 0	—4
Reds	0 0 0	0 0 0	—0

★ 3 ★

Push Comes to Shove

On Wednesday the Dodgers played the A's, and they had no trouble. They won, 14 to 2. The coach let the rookies, Anthony and Ben, play the whole game, and they both got hits.

Harlan also played catcher all six innings, and he was starting to feel more confident that he could play the position.

Lian's first three times up he took his usual smooth stroke. But the fourth time, once the Dodgers had their big lead, Harlan could tell that he tried to go for the fences.

He got under the ball and popped it up, and he was mad again. Harlan knew he still wanted that homer.

On the next Saturday the Dodgers played
the Padres. The game got off to a good start.
Lian made a great play in the first inning
to keep the Padres from getting a run, and
then he led off with a nice single in the bottom of the inning.

The team batted around that inning, and
Lian ended up getting a second hit to drive
in two runs.

The Padres played better after that first
inning, but at the end of five, the Dodgers
were ahead, 8 to 2. All the Dodgers had to
do was get the Padres out one more time.

If they won, they would be 8 and 1, and
they would play the Giants for the second-
half championship in the next game—the
last game of the regular season.

Maybe the Dodgers thought they had it
made. Or maybe Eddie Boschi's arm got
tired. But just when the game seemed to be
wrapped up, some pretty weak Padres' batters banged out hits. Two runs scored, and
with only one out, the top of the order was
coming up.

It was time to get serious and get these
guys out.

Coach Wilkens talked to Eddie, and then decided to bring Kenny in to take his place on the mound. Eddie moved out to left field, and Jonathan came in to play shortstop.

Kenny looked good warming up, and his first pitch *popped* into Harlan's glove. Lundberg, the Padres' second baseman, was used to Eddie's fastballs. He swung late on Kenny's first pitch.

He swung late on the next pitch, too, but he managed to tick the ball and roll it down the first-base line.

The ball died halfway to the bag—a perfect bunt, even if it was an accident. And Lundberg was on.

Now there were runners at first and second and still only one out. The Padres' best two batters were coming up. Ben and Anthony were in the game now, so the Dodgers' defense wasn't at its strongest.

But Kenny looked sharp, and the Dodgers still had a good lead. They could get two outs.

Things looked better when Jorgensen, the girl who played left field, slapped a hard grounder at Henry, at third.

Henry made a great pickup, and now he only had to get to the bag to make the force at third. But as he tried to set his foot, his shoe slipped and he crashed on his chest.

He scrambled up and dove at the bag, just as the runner was sliding in. At the same time the home plate umpire was running up the line to see the play.

"Safe!!!"

Harlan thought Henry had gotten the guy, but he was a long way from the play, so he kept his mouth shut. It was Jonathan who lost his cool.

"You gotta be kidding, ump!" he yelled. "That wasn't even close. Henry's glove was on the bag first!"

"You play baseball," the umpire said. "I'll call the outs." He turned around and walked away.

"Well, you can't even *see*, so how are you going to do that?"

The umpire spun around. "Listen, kid," he said, "I'm going to pretend that I can't *hear*. I ought to boot you out of this game right now. You keep quiet, or I'll do just that."

But Jonathan wasn't finished. He went

striding after the umpire. "Can't you ask the other ump? You couldn't see the tag from there."

Lian grabbed Jonathan, and tried to hold him from walking any closer. But Jonathan pushed Lian away.

The umpire stopped and turned around again. "I saw it fine. Now that's the *last* I'm going to hear from you."

"I don't see why I can't—"

Clamp.

Lian suddenly reached up and clasped his hand around Jonathan's mouth. "Don't say any more," he told Jonathan.

But Jonathan *really* didn't like that. He pushed Lian away and shouted, "Quit that, you little shrimp!"

"Don't get thrown out!" Lian said. "Don't be stupid."

"Don't call *me* stupid," Jonathan said, and he stepped forward and gave Lian a shove.

Lian was caught off guard, and he went stumbling backward and landed on his seat.

Harlan ran to get between Jonathan and Lian. "Come on, Jonathan," he said. "Don't blow it."

By now the Padres were really enjoying

this. "Hey, don't beat up on that little boy!" Hugh Roberts yelled.

But Coach Wilkens grabbed Jonathan by the shoulder. "Jonathan, that's enough!" he said.

Jonathan spun around. "Coach, he was *out!*" he shouted.

"No, he wasn't. The umpire called him safe."

"But Henry's glove was already on the bag. I *saw* it."

"I know. So did I. But we don't make the call. The umpire does. Now calm down and play ball. I'd take you out of the game myself, but I've used all my substitutes."

Jonathan slammed his fist into his glove and then spun and walked back to his position. "*Okay.* Let's get these guys."

Lian had gotten up. But he stood looking at the coach. Harlan wondered what he was thinking.

"I'm sorry, Lian," the coach said.

Lian didn't move. Some of the Padres were still yelling smart remarks about Jonathan picking on him. But Lian was now looking toward the sidelines. Lian's father had come down out of the bleachers. He was calling to Lian in Chinese.

"Let's get them out now," the coach said.

Lian took another look at his father, and then he shook his head and said, "No, father." Finally he turned and walked back to his position, but Harlan could see that he was *very* upset.

Roberts was up to bat—the best hitter on the Padres' team.

And now the bases were loaded.

Jonathan was still mad. Kenny's concentration was shot. And Lian didn't look as if he was playing baseball. He was just standing in the field, filling up the space.

Harlan saw real trouble ahead.

Roberts seemed to see what was going on too. He swung and missed on Kenny's first pitch, but he had tried to push the ball to the right side—where Lian was still standing, unready.

Roberts took a pitch inside after that, but on the next pitch he hit the ball sharply on the ground to Lian's right.

But Lian's reactions kicked in. He attacked the ball. He backhanded it, and in one quick motion dug the ball from his glove and flipped it, underhand, toward second.

Jonathan had charged the bag, and the throw was perfect.

He took the ball in stride, tagged the bag, and made a perfect throw to first.

Bang! Bang!

Double play!

The game was over and . . .

Wait a minute! The umpire was yelling that the runner was safe at second.

Jonathan had missed the bag with his foot.

Before the Dodgers realized what had happened, two runs had scored, and the other runner had gone all the way to third.

And Jonathan was going crazy. But this time it was Sterling who grabbed him and made him shut up. And Sterling was big enough to do it.

Lian simply stood and watched—except that Harlan saw him shake his head as if to say, "I don't understand this."

The Dodgers had to dig in all over again. Brenchley, the catcher, was coming up, and the lead was now down to two runs.

Kenny took a deep breath, let it out, hesitated, and then fired a hard, low fastball.

Brenchley whacked it on the ground, right at Lian.

Lian charged the ball, picked it up—smooth as if he were on skates—and he threw out the runner by a couple of steps.

Easy!

Or at least Lian made it look that way.

And now the Dodgers could celebrate for real. They would be playing for the second-half championship on Wednesday night!

But while the players ran to each other, slapped hands, and shouted their congratulations, Lian was leaving. He had tossed out the runner, trotted off the field, and never stopped.

Harlan was the only one who seemed to notice, and he ran after him. Lian was walking toward his parents, who were waiting just outside the fence.

"Lian," Harlan yelled, but Lian wouldn't look back. When Harlan caught up, he got in front of him and made him stop. "Lian, it's okay now. Jonathan just has a bad temper. He didn't mean to push you. Let's go back and talk to him."

"No!" Lian said. And nothing else.

He stepped around Harlan and walked

to his parents. They all began to talk in Chinese, and Lian's parents appeared to be just as unhappy and upset as he was.

Harlan wondered whether Lian would quit the Dodgers.

BOX SCORE, GAME 18

Angel Park Dodgers 14   **Paseo A's 2**

	ab	r	h	rbi		ab	r	h	rbi
Jie 2b	4	2	2	1	Oshima 2b	3	1	0	0
White 3b	4	2	2	2	Santos 1b	3	1	1	1
Sandoval p	5	2	2	2	De Klein cf	2	0	1	0
Swingle ss	4	2	2	2	Smith c	2	0	1	1
Malone cf	4	1	2	2	Chavez p	3	0	1	0
Sloan c	4	2	2	0	Powell 3b	2	0	0	0
Scott rf	3	1	2	2	Watrous rf	3	0	1	0
Ruiz 1b	3	0	1	0	Naile ss	2	0	0	0
Riddle lf	3	1	2	1	Sullivan lf	3	0	1	0
Roper 1b	1	1	1	0	Henegan cf	1	0	0	0
Bacon lf	1	0	1	1	Trout 3b	1	0	0	0
Boschi 2b	1	0	0	0	Reilly ss	1	0	1	0
ttl	37	14	19	13		26	2	7	2

Dodgers 2 0 9 1 1 1—14
A's   0 0 2 0 0 0—2

BOX SCORE, GAME 19

Santa Rita Padres 6

	ab	r	h	rbi
Lundberg 2b	4	2	2	0
Jorgensen lf	4	0	1	1
Roberts p	4	0	2	1
Brenchley c	4	0	1	0
Durkin 1b	2	0	2	0
Blough 3b	3	1	1	0
Palmer ss	3	1	1	1
Campbell cf	1	0	0	0
Orosco rf	0	1	0	0
Valenciano rf	2	0	0	0
Nakatani 1b	1	0	0	0
Rollins cf	2	1	1	1
ttl	30	6	11	4

Angel Park Dodgers 8

	ab	r	h	rbi
Jie 2b	4	1	3	2
White 3b	4	2	2	0
Sandoval ss, p	4	1	1	2
Swingle lf, ss	3	2	3	2
Malone cf	3	0	2	1
Roper 1b	2	1	1	0
Scott rf	2	0	0	0
Bacon c	2	1	1	1
Boschi p, lf	2	0	1	0
Sloan c	1	0	0	0
Ruiz lf	1	0	0	0
Riddle 2b	1	0	0	0
	29	8	14	8

Padres	0 0 2	0 0 4	—6
Dodgers	6 0 0	2 0 x	—8

★ **4** ★

Little Giant

Harlan talked to the coach about Lian. Coach Wilkens said he would go visit with Lian and his parents.

On Monday, after school, the Dodgers held a practice. But before the practice started, Coach Wilkens talked to Harlan.

"It was hard," the coach said. "Lian speaks better English than his parents. They kept saying that Lian had been 'shamed' in front of everyone. I guess they were talking about the fact that Jonathan knocked him down."

"Did you tell them that Jonathan just lost his temper?"

"Yeah, but I'm not sure they understood. Lian said, 'I promised to play, so I will play,' but he's sure unhappy."

After that, the coach called everyone together, and he talked about supporting each
other. The big games were coming up, and
everyone had to feel good about each other.

"I understand why Jonathan got upset the
other day," Coach Wilkens told the players.
"Henry really did get his glove on the bag
first. But the thing is, an ump is going to
make some mistakes. It doesn't do any good
to argue a judgment call like that. He's not
going to change his mind."

Jonathan nodded, and he did appear to
be sorry for what he had done.

"But that wasn't the worst thing,
Jonathan," Coach Wilkens added. "Lian was
just trying to keep you from getting thrown
out of the game. You really owe him an
apology."

That seemed to embarrass Jonathan. He
nodded again, but he didn't say anything.

"Let's hear it," the coach said.

The players were sitting on the grass in a
half circle. Lian was sitting straight across
from Jonathan. Jonathan looked at him and
said, "Hey, I'm sorry, little guy. I didn't
mean anything. I was just mad." He laughed.

But Harlan knew Jonathan had said the wrong thing. Lian's face was stern, and it didn't change.

Coach Wilkens must have seen it too. "Let's lay off the 'little guy' stuff. Lian may be smaller than you, but he plays like a giant."

"I hope not," Billy said. "He better play like a Dodger. We gotta *beat* the Giants— *twice*."

The players laughed, and so did Coach Wilkens. "Well, you know what I mean," he said. And then he changed the subject. He told the players to relax and play their best. He felt sure they could win.

And so practice began, and everyone worked hard.

Harlan watched Lian. He practiced hard, but he didn't say anything to anyone. He had always smiled and been friendly, but the smile was gone now.

When Wednesday came, Lian still wasn't smiling, but he looked determined when he stepped up to bat.

He started out the game by watching one of Hausberg's big curves break outside. Lian almost never swung at a bad pitch, but he had to stop himself at the last second this time.

"Throw strikes," Dave Weight yelled from third base. "This little kid can't hit."

Everyone in the league knew that Lian *could* hit. It was just the kind of stuff guys yelled during the games. But Lian stepped out of the box, turned around, and stared at Weight.

All that did was let the Giants know that they were getting to him. They all started working on him. And the word "little" was in everything they said.

Coach Wilkens suddenly called time-out, and he trotted down the line toward Lian. "Don't worry about all that stuff," he called to Lian. "Just get on base, okay?"

Harlan watched Lian take a breath and settle himself down. He stepped back into the box, let a fastball go by, and then waited on one of big "House" Hausberg's curves. He took his good stroke and drove the ball straight through the middle.

Harlan watched Lian scoot to first and take his turn. He made a fake toward second, to try to get the outfielder to throw behind him, but then he retreated to first. He was always thinking, always watching for a chance.

Glenn, the first baseman, yelled to Hausberg. "Okay, the little guy lucked out. But we can get these other guys."

Harlan saw Lian give Glenn a hard look. Then he planted his foot on first base and got ready to go.

But Henry flied out. And Kenny hit a grounder to short. Lian was forced at second. Jonathan came up then and hit a long bomb, but it wasn't quite long enough, and the left fielder chased it down.

Jonathan marched out to the mound and pitched a perfect first inning of his own. His fastball was humming, and he struck out all three batters.

The pitching duel was on.

The only hit in the first three innings was the one that Lian had gotten. In the fourth, Kenny and Jonathan both hit singles, but Hausberg settled down and got out of the inning.

So as the Giants came up in the bottom

of the fourth, neither team had scored, and a whole season was riding on these last couple of innings.

Jonathan had to face Weight to start off the inning, and he was one guy who didn't let Jonathan's fastball scare him.

When he came to bat, the whole Giant team was screaming. They hadn't had a hit yet, and they knew it was their star player who had to get something going.

Jonathan knew it too, and he was careful. He tried to move in and out and catch the corners, but he ended up with a 3 and 1 count, and then he had to make sure he threw a strike. He let go with a powerful fastball, but Weight was ready.

Crack!!!

There was no question about it. As soon as Harlan heard the sound he knew. The ball soared way . . . *way* . . . over the left field fence.

The Giants had the lead, 1 to 0.

Lots of people had come from Blue Springs, and they were going crazy. Harlan looked around at his parents, who were sitting in the bleachers behind the Dodgers' dugout. "Don't worry," Harlan's mother shouted. "You can get that run back."

Or at least that's what Harlan thought she said. It was hard to tell with all the noise.

What worried Harlan was Jonathan. He was a great athlete, but he couldn't always keep his control. Too often he would pitch great until something like this happened, and then he would try to make up for it and only pitch worse.

But Jenny jogged over to the mound and said something to Jonathan. He nodded, and then Jenny yelled to her teammates, "Okay. We're still going to get these guys!"

The infield talked it up, and Jonathan went back to the pitching rubber. He looked smooth when he delivered the pitch, and it was a *fireball*.

Glenn swung late and fouled the pitch off.

Then he swung over the next pitch and topped it. The ball rolled slowly to the right side. Jonathan tried to get to it, but the ball took a funny spin and kicked under his glove.

Harlan muttered, "Oh no!"

The Dodgers didn't need that kind of bad break right now when . . .

But then, there was Lian, charging, backing up Jonathan. He made the pickup and flipped the ball, underhand, across his body to Jenny.

The ball popped into her glove, just as the runner crossed the bag.

Harlan's breath stopped, but then the umpire's arm shot up.

Out!!!

It was the lift the team needed right then. Instead of a runner on and no outs, the bases were clear. Jonathan put down the next two batters, and the Dodgers were out of the inning.

Now they had two chances to come back.

This was going to get tense.

"Harlan," the coach yelled, "bat for Billy. You're up first."

Harlan had known that was coming, but he still felt his stomach take a little flip.

Lian and Jonathan were just walking into the dugout. "Great play!" Jonathan said, and he patted Lian on the shoulder. A couple of the players slapped hands with Lian.

"Thank you," Lian said. "Thank you." And Harlan noticed that he was smiling just a little.

This was good. This was exactly what . . .

And then Jonathan said, "When you get up, punch another little single, and then *I'll* knock one into orbit. We're going to *get these guys!*"

Everyone in the dugout roared, and Billy yelled, "That's right. *Swat* is going to *swat* one out of here."

Lian walked to the bench and sat down. Harlan followed him. He was about to tell Lian not to let Jonathan bother him, but Lian spoke first. "Maybe *he* hits a home run," he said. "Maybe I do."

★ 5 ★

Home-Run Swing

Harlan walked to the batter's box. But he heard Lian call, and he turned around.

Lian motioned him closer, and Harlan walked back. "I watched the pitcher, Hausberg. I saw something. His shoulder comes down a little when he throws a curve ball. Watch. You can tell."

"Thanks, Lian," Harlan said, but he wasn't sure the information would help him until it was too late.

Harlan wanted to take a couple of pitches and see what Lian was talking about. But the first pitch was a fastball, low in the strike zone. Strike one.

Harlan took the next pitch—a curve—and

he did see the difference. But the curve caught the inside corner for a strike.

Now he was in trouble, with an 0 and 2 count.

Michael Wilkens chewed Harlan out a little for not swinging, but Harlan looked at Lian, and Lian nodded.

Now Harlan had to come through.

He watched Hausberg's motion. The shoulder didn't drop. Fastball. But the pitch was outside.

And then on the next pitch Harlan saw Hausberg's shoulder come down and he read "curve ball," even though the pitch came straight at him. He hung in, concentrated, and *met* the curve as it broke.

The ball clicked—*solid*—and shot off his bat past the third baseman and into left field.

The Dodgers all shouted as Harlan raced toward first. He took a turn and thought about going, but Michael Wilkens was yelling, "Hold up. Hold up."

Eddie Boschi was coming up next, and Lian was on deck.

Harlan saw Lian tell Eddie about Hausberg's motion.

But Eddie got too anxious. He may have seen that the curve was coming, but he jumped at the pitch and sent a slow roller straight back to Hausberg.

Big House fielded the ball and threw Eddie out, but Harlan moved to second.

The tying run was in scoring position, and Lian was probably the best batter to have up. He knew what to look for, and he could push a single into right field so Harlan could score.

Just as he stepped up to bat, Jonathan yelled, "Keep it going, Lian. Get on base. I'll bring everybody in."

At the same moment, the Giants' coach yelled to his outfielders, "Come in closer," and he waved them toward the infield.

Lian stepped up to the plate and dug in.

The first pitch was a fastball, low, and Lian let it go by.

"Just *poke* one, Lian," Coach Wilkens yelled.

But Hausberg threw his curve, and Lian was waiting. He swung with everything he had, and *blasted* the ball into left field.

It was a long one!

The left fielder had to turn his back to the infield and run as hard as he could go.

But the ball was hit high, and the fielder got under it. He was standing right in front of the fence when he made the catch.

Lian had come close. He had almost put his team ahead.

But it was still an out.

Lian had run halfway to first base. He stopped and kicked the dirt when he saw the ball hadn't made it.

Harlan was still at second and worried he might get stranded there. But Henry drove the ball into center field for a single, and Harlan roared around third and scored.

With Kenny and Jonathan coming up, it just might be the time for the Dodgers to get a real rally going.

And Kenny gave it a shot.

He hit the ball sharply, but Weight stabbed it, and then made a good, long throw for the out.

The game was going to the bottom of the fifth, tied 1 to 1.

What Harlan wanted was a one-two-three inning and then a chance for his team to get some more runs in the sixth.

Hausberg was up. He wasn't the greatest hitter in the world, but when he connected, he could hit the ball a country mile. And he looked ready to do just that.

Harlan had an idea. He called for a change-up on the first pitch. Kenny had just come in the game, and he had been warming up with nothing but fastballs. House would be looking for some heat.

But Kenny shook the call off.

Harlan called, "Time out" and ran out to the mound.

"Let's waste a fastball outside, first, to get him looking for speed," Kenny said. "And then come with the change."

"That's what we usually do. Maybe we should try to cross him up."

Kenny thought for a couple of seconds, and then he nodded and said, "Okay. Let's do it."

Harlan ran back, and Kenny fired hard— but used his change-up grip. Hausberg unloaded, but he was way out in front. He ticked the ball off the end of his bat.

Kenny threw him out, and then he grinned at Harlan. "Good thinking," he yelled.

The next two batters were substitutes, and not very good hitters. Kenny struck out the first one, and got the other on a soft grounder.

And now this was it.

Sixth inning.

A whole season, everything the team had worked for, could hang on these next six outs—three by each team. Or would it go to extra innings? That would mean new pitchers, since Little League only allowed a player to pitch six innings a week.

Jonathan was leading off, and Jenny and Sterling would follow. They were all strong hitters. And the word had spread about Hausberg's shoulder dropping when he threw a curve.

Jonathan dug in, and he played it smart. He let a couple of sucker pitches go by, and then he got a sweet pitch over the plate. He just met the pitch and socked a nice line drive. The ball whistled over the shortstop's head.

And it kept going!

Jonathan had gotten *all* of it. And the ball carried straight as a rope, over the left fielder's head and right at the fence.

Harlan thought it would be off the fence for extra bases, but it . . . disappeared.

It couldn't have. . . .

And yet, the ump was waving his arm around.

HOME RUN!

The Dodgers had the *lead!*

Jonathan was as surprised as anyone. He forgot his home-run trot and ran fast all the way.

The whole team ran out to meet him at the plate.

After that, Jenny slapped a single and so did Malone. And then Jacob laid down a perfect bunt to move them over. And Harlan poked a nice single to score *two more runs.*

The team was going crazy and screaming for more.

Eddie hit the ball hard too, but the first baseman made a good stop on it. Still, Harlan moved to second.

Lian was coming up with a chance to drive in another run.

But on the first pitch he took a wild, hard swing . . . and missed.

"No, Lian. Let's see that good swing of yours," the coach was yelling.

But Lian didn't listen. He swung just as hard at Hausberg's curve. And he lifted a harmless fly to left field.

The rally was over. What was Lian trying to do?

Still, the Dodgers had a three-run lead. They only needed to survive the bottom of the sixth.

What worried Harlan, though, was that the Giants had their best hitters coming up. And they weren't going to give up without a fight.

Kenny was in a groove, though, and he made a fool of Nugent, the left fielder. He moved the ball in and out, up and down, changed speeds, and finally struck him out on a *hot* fastball.

He did almost the same to Sanchez, the shortstop. But Sanchez got enough wood on the ball to roll a grounder to Jenny at first.

Two outs.

And Weight was coming up. He couldn't win the game with a single stroke, but he could keep the game going, and he could keep the Giants' hopes alive.

Kenny went with his best stuff—his fast-

ball and his good curve. The two great athletes battled, and Weight fouled a couple off,
but finally he spanked one hard to the right
side. Jenny took a couple of quick steps and
dove, but the ball was past her.

Lian darted to his left and dove too, and
he managed to knock the ball down. He
scrambled up and grabbed it. And then he
spun and fired the ball hard.

Too hard and too late!

The ball whistled by Jenny, wide of her
reach. Weight trotted over to second.

Harlan shook his head. It was a dumb
play. But worse than that, it wasn't Lian. He
was always the one who kept his head in
tight situations.

But Glenn, the first baseman, made it easy
on the Dodgers. He went after an outside
pitch and popped it up in foul territory.
Jenny got under the ball, near the fence,
and she kept her concentration—even with
all the Giants screaming.

She squeezed the ball, and it was all over.

The Dodgers had won the second-half
championship.

One more win, and they could win it all!

Harlan felt great.

Almost.

There was something gnawing at him. Somehow the team needed to get the old Lian back if they were going to beat the Giants one more time.

BOX SCORE, GAME 20

Angel Park Dodgers 4

	ab	r	h	rbi
Jie 2b	4	0	1	0
White 3b	3	0	1	1
Sandoval ss, p	3	0	1	0
Swingle p, ss	3	1	2	1
Roper 1b	2	1	1	0
Malone cf	3	1	1	0
Scott rf	1	0	0	0
Bacon c	1	0	0	0
Boschi lf	3	0	0	0
Ruiz 1b	1	0	0	0
Riddle 2b	1	0	0	0
Sloan c	2	1	2	2
ttl	27	4	9	4

Blue Springs Giants 1

	ab	r	h	rbi
Nugent lf	3	0	0	0
Sanchez ss	3	0	0	0
Weight 3b	2	1	2	1
Glenn 1b	3	0	0	0
Cooper 2b	1	0	0	0
Spinner cf	2	0	0	0
Hausberg p	2	0	0	0
Dodero c	1	0	0	0
Waganheim rf	0	0	0	0
Zonn rf	1	0	0	0
Villareal lf	1	0	0	0
Stevens cf	1	0	0	0
	20	1	2	1

Dodgers   0 0 0   0 1 3—4
Giants   0 0 0   1 0 0—1

★ 6 ★

Getting Taller

On Thursday the Dodgers had a practice scheduled. Harlan spread the word at school for everyone to come early. He and the coach had been cooking up an idea.

The players were glad to show up. School would soon be out for the summer, and kids were restless. With the play-off on Saturday, all the players had baseball on their minds.

As the Dodgers arrived they started throwing balls around. But then Harlan said, "Hey, everyone, come over here. The coach asked me to talk to you about something."

Jonathan was the only one who said, "Why *you?*"

Harlan paid no attention. "He thought it would be good if we got together to work on some mistakes we've been making."

"Oh, sure," Jonathan said, "and *you're* going to show us?"

"No. But an expert has been watching our games, and he's noticed some mistakes. I want him to give us some advice."

"So where is he?" Billy asked.

"Oh, he's here." Harlan grinned, and he waited a couple of seconds, and then he said, "Come up, Mr. Jie."

The players didn't complain. They liked Lian. But some of the kids laughed.

Lian looked confused, but he came forward.

"Okay, Lian," Harlan said, "just tell them—or show them—some of the stuff you've mentioned to me."

Lian stared at Harlan. He didn't say a word.

"Remember what you told me about making throws from the outfield?"

Lian didn't respond for a time, and Harlan started to get worried, and then Lian finally said, very softly, "If a runner goes around a base—"

"Speak up, Lian. I can't hear you," Sterling said, from the back of the group. All the kids were sitting on the grass.

"Okay." Lian swallowed, and Harlan could tell how nervous he was.

As Harlan watched from behind, Lian didn't seem much like an expert. With his shirt tucked in, only half his number 9 showed up. It looked like a zero. And his cap was adjusted to the smallest size—and was still too big for him.

"In one of our games a runner ran too far around first base and—"

"He did what?" Jonathan asked.

Harlan could see that Jonathan was not going to make this easy—even though he knew that English was difficult for Lian, or maybe *because* he knew English was difficult for Lian.

Harlan tried to explain. "A runner on another team rounded first and started toward second, but then he held up."

"Yes," Lian said. "Jacob was in right field. He throws to first and the runner goes to second."

"I know," Jacob said. "I should've thrown to second."

"Yes. But not so soon. Always—if a runner stops, and you don't know which way he goes—run *to* him."

"What?" Jonathan asked.

"You run straight at him," Harlan said. "And you don't throw the ball until he commits himself. Sometimes you can freeze him. If he breaks for first, *then* you can throw behind him and maybe get him."

"Who doesn't know that?" Jonathan said. "I learned that my first year in Little League."

"Yeah, the coach taught me that," Jacob said. "I just wasn't thinking."

"Well, okay, but that's the kind of stuff we need to remember on Saturday."

This wasn't going the way Harlan had hoped. Lian looked more uncomfortable than ever.

"There's some other stuff," Harlan said. "Remember that double play we messed up against the Padres? Lian knows a better way to—"

"I didn't mess up. The ump missed the call," Jonathan said.

"Maybe. But Lian showed me the footwork he uses to make that play. Let him show you."

Jonathan mumbled, but he walked out on the diamond. Now Lian didn't have to talk so much, and he could demonstrate.

He had Henry hit a ground ball to Ben Riddle, who made the toss to second. Lian showed the players how he caught the ball as he stepped over the bag with his left foot and dragged his right foot across the base.

"No one slides into your foot this way. And you don't have to look down to see the base," he told them. He repeated the move three times, and then he asked Kenny to try it.

Kenny caught on quickly. He tried it a couple of times, and then he said, "That's beautiful. No one ever showed me that before." He turned and looked at Jonathan. "Try it," he said.

"Hey, that's the way I already do it," Jonathan said. He stood with his hands on his hips.

It was a bad moment, and Harlan thought he had blown the whole thing. But Kenny didn't blink. "No it isn't, Jonathan. You missed the bag that day because you stabbed at it. This way, you drag across, and you keep your eye on your throw."

Jonathan didn't like that. But just as he was about to react, Henry said, "Kenny's right, Jonathan. Listen to Lian. The guy learned good baseball in Taiwan. It doesn't matter how big he is. He knows what he's doing."

Jonathan's mouth was still open. Harlan could see that he was trying to decide what he was going to say. What finally came out was, "Hey, I like Lian. He's a good player."

"That's right," Henry said. "And he *knows* the game."

"Hey, I know that."

"Just try the footwork the way he does it," Harlan said.

By now Jonathan almost *had* to show that he was willing to listen. And so he tried the technique a couple of times. "Yeah, that does work," he finally said, and he sort of shrugged. "I was doing it . . . a little different from that."

Lian nodded and he smiled.

Jonathan smiled too. "Hey, look, Lian, I didn't mean anything by calling you 'little.' Okay?"

"Okay."

But Lian wasn't finished. He had noticed other things. He showed the players how to shorten their strokes, especially with two strikes, and get better bat control. He also talked to them about hitting the ball behind the runners so they could advance on the base paths.

And he had specific suggestions for some players. Anthony sometimes threw the ball with his weight on his front foot.

Eddie Boschi had gotten back to his habit of pitching too much with his arm and not using his legs and body.

Kenny wasn't catching his balance very well after his pitches, so he was not ready to make fielding plays.

Jacob was looping his bat at the beginning of his swing, and that was slowing down his stroke.

It was all sort of amazing. The more Lian showed the players, the more they could see just how well he understood the game. And everything he showed them seemed to work.

Before long, players were asking him questions. Jenny had him show her how he handled hard-hit grounders when they came straight at him. And Sterling wanted to know how to deal with a high fly hit into the sun.

And Lian knew the answers.

"Man, oh man," Anthony said. "They must have great coaches in Taiwan."

Lian smiled. "Yes. And players listen. The Dodgers have a great coach too. But sometimes players here don't listen."

Everyone had to agree.

But they had listened today. "This stuff is really going to help us," Jenny told Lian.

And Jonathan seemed to sense that it was time for him to make things right. "Hey, Lian," he said, "you're a good, smart player. It doesn't matter how tall you are."

Lian liked that. He even nodded to Jonathan—sort of bowed.

And Jonathan nodded back.

Harlan said, "But, Lian, I want to teach *you* one thing too."

"Oh, good," Lian said.

"Don't try to hit homers. That's not what you do best."

"Yes, I know," Lian said. "I learned this lesson myself." And he smiled that old smile that Harlan hadn't seen for a while.

Winner Takes All

This was it.

One big game.

The winners would be the champs for the whole season, and they would get to play in the district tournament.

Back at the first of the season, the Dodgers had vowed they would go all the way this time and win the district tournament. But right now they had to get past the Giants— one more time.

The coach talked to the players before the game. "Let's relax and enjoy this," he told them. "Don't get yourselves all uptight and worried."

"I'm not worried," Billy said. "The Giants aren't so tough when big House isn't pitching."

"Well, I don't know," Coach Wilkens answered. "This Glenn kid is pitching today, and he's been pitching better all year. I watched him the other day against the A's, and he was really *zipping* his fastball. He has good control, too."

"Lian noticed something about Glenn that we ought to watch," Harlan said.

"What's that, Lian?"

"He throws fastballs. No curve balls," Lian said. "He has a change-up, but many times he does the same thing. He throws two, maybe three fastballs, and then comes the change-up."

"Okay," the coach said. "That's a good thing to be aware of. But we can't stand there and take too many pitches. He stays in the strike zone most of the time. But if he throws a couple of fastballs, look for that change."

"We're going to *murder* him!" Jonathan yelled.

"Now wait a minute. Let's not start bragging. Let's show some class. No mouthing off." The coach was looking right at Jonathan. "This could end up a close game, and if it does, it's the team that plays smart that will win it."

And so the Dodgers took the field. They were excited, but Harlan could also feel the confidence.

Of course, the Giants were confident too, and they weren't going to be easy to beat twice in one week.

They proved that in the very first inning.

Nugent, the left fielder, fouled off a couple of pitches and finally worked Kenny for a walk.

Kenny seemed a little nervous, but he settled down and got Cooper to hit a ground ball to Jonathan at short. Lian took the throw for the force at second.

That brought up Dave Weight. Kenny took a long breath and then fired a perfect fastball on the outside corner at the knees. Not many guys could hit that pitch, but Weight slapped it to right field.

The ball arched just over Lian's out-stretched glove.

The runner had to wait to see if Lian would catch it, so he only made it to second.

But that meant runners were at first and second with only one out.

"Hey, little kid," one of the Giants yelled, "if you were the size of a *real* player, you would have caught it."

But the Giant coach was quick to call from the coach's box, "That's enough of that."

Harlan wasn't in the game yet. He was standing in the dugout, his fingers gripping the chain-link fence. He hoped that Lian wouldn't let stuff like that bother him.

But he didn't have to wonder about it long.

Glenn, the left-hander, was up. He swung at the first pitch and laced it hard to right field. Lian reacted like a coiled spring. He leaped—twisting and stretching—and he snagged the ball.

As he touched the ground he was already

spinning the rest of the way around so that he could shoot the ball to Jenny.

And his instinct was right.

Weight had thought the ball was going through and had broken from the bag. By the time he could put on the brakes, the ball was popping into Jenny's glove.

Double play.

A noise rushed through the crowd—a giant *aaahhhh*—and it was followed by big cheers. Lots of people were at the game, and they knew a great play when they saw it. Even the Giants' fans applauded.

Lian trotted back to the dugout. His teammates all slapped him on the back, or slapped hands with him. And Billy couldn't resist. "How *tall* did you say he had to be?" he yelled across to the Giants, who were taking the field.

No one answered.

Coach Wilkens walked over to the dugout and looked at his players. "Now *that* is what I mean about playing smart. Lian knew where he was going to throw the ball the second he caught it."

Lian said nothing. He got his bat and walked out toward the plate. He watched Glenn warm up, and he timed his practice swings to the pitches.

Then he stepped to the plate. He took a fastball over the plate, and then he took one outside. One more down the middle, and Coach Wilkens was yelling, "Be a hitter, Lian. Come on."

But the next pitch was the change-up, and Lian was ready. He punched it to left field over the head of the leaping shortstop. The kid was taller than Lian—but not tall enough. Lian had done what he did best—get on base.

Henry did the same thing. He took a couple of pitches, and then he got the change-up. He knocked it into center field for a single. Lian got a good jump and used his speed to scoot all the way to third.

Kenny was up, and Jonathan was on deck. Now was the time to get some early runs. Glenn fired a couple of fastballs for strikes. And Kenny didn't swing.

Kenny couldn't let any more go by, but

when he got a third fastball outside, he knew
he could expect the change-up.

And he got it.

He socked the ball hard to left-center, and
the ball rolled through the gap. Two runs
scored, and Kenny had himself a double.

But the Giants' coach wasted no time
running to the mound.

Coach Wilkens walked over and talked to
Jonathan, and then he looked in the dugout and said, "They know what we were
doing—sitting on his change. We won't get
away with it anymore. Look for fastballs."

And he was right. Jonathan got nothing
but fastballs, and some good ones. He hit
the ball hard on the ground to third, and
Weight looked Kenny back to second and
then threw Jonathan out.

Jenny flied out to right, and Sterling flied
to left, and that was the inning. But the
Dodgers had a two-run lead, and Lian's
knowledge had paid off again.

Kenny was pitching tough, and the team
kept playing great defense. Sterling ran
down a long fly in center, and Jenny made

a great stop on a ball that Henry threw in the dirt.

After three innings, the Dodgers hadn't given up a run.

The only trouble was, Glenn was now looking like King Kong out there, throwing almost all fastballs—and *screamers*. In the second and third innings, no one had a hit off him.

Kenny got the Giants out in the fourth— although he had a little more trouble. He walked Weight. And Henry had to make a great play on a hard-hit liner that Sanchez hit.

In the bottom of the inning, Anthony came in for Jacob and struck out swinging. Harlan took over for Billy and grounded out. And Ben watched a 3 and 2 pitch hit the outside corner for strike three.

Kenny looked good again in the fifth. He was throwing hard, and his control was nearly perfect. He did give up a second hit, but his shutout was still alive.

This was not going to be easy. The game was coming down to the end, and the Giants had a lot of pride. They weren't going to give up without a fight.

The butterflies were going crazy in Harlan's stomach.

★ 8 ★

Final Inning

Harlan still felt the Dodgers might need more runs before they were finished. And now was the time to do it. Lian was leading off.

It was the bottom of the fifth inning. If the Dodgers could keep their lead, they wouldn't bat in the sixth.

Glenn was popping his fastball, but he had begun to use his change-up more often again. He was even trying his curve. And it wasn't much of a pitch. Too bad the Dodgers didn't know when it was coming the way they did against Hausberg.

"Come on, Lian!" Jenny shouted. "Get on base!"

Lian pumped his fist and nodded at Jenny. He stepped to the plate and took a *hard* practice swing.

But when the pitch came in, Lian squared off to bunt. The pitch was inside, and Lian had to twist away from it.

Weight charged in from third base when he saw Lian try to bunt. Now he stayed on the infield grass in case he tried it again.

Glenn reared back and let go with a zinger of a fastball, and Lian squared around once more.

Weight charged.

Just then Lian stepped back and swung. He chopped the ball sharply down the line. Weight dove, but the ball got by him. The fake had worked!

Once again, a buzz went through the crowd. It was a smart play, and not an easy one to pull off.

Henry checked Coach Wilkens's signals. And then he, too, squared around. Weight didn't charge quite as hard this time, and Henry laid down a good bunt for the sacrifice.

Lian moved to second.

Kenny would now get his chance to build the lead.

But it didn't happen. He took a couple of fastballs outside, and then swung at a curve. The ball didn't break much, but Kenny swung early and rolled a grounder to the shortstop.

The shortstop almost threw the ball away, but big Hausberg was playing first today, and he reached high and got it.

So there were two outs, and Lian was still at second.

Jonathan walked to the batter's box. But before he could step to the plate, Lian yelled for a time-out. He ran in to talk to Jonathan.

Harlan wondered what was going on.

Jonathan nodded a few times, and then he went back to the plate. The first pitch was right where he liked it, belt high, but Jonathan didn't swing.

Harlan knew something was up.

The next pitch was another fastball, but it was a little low, and then Glenn threw one outside. All fastballs.

Jonathan seemed to be champing at the

bit. The next pitch was hard down the middle again, but he still let it go by.

Harlan hoped Jonathan wouldn't end up striking out. The coach was yelling to him to be ready this time.

But when Jonathan got set this time, Harlan noticed that he was watching Lian, not the pitcher. Then Harlan saw Lian reach up and touch his own shoulder, and Jonathan nodded. The pitch was a curve, slow and hanging over the plate.

Jonathan seemed to be expecting it. He hammered the pitch into center field and Lian scored.

The Dodgers all rushed out to slap hands with Lian as he crossed the plate. But they were still yelling, "Let's get some more runs. Jenny, bring Jonathan home."

When Jenny dropped a little fly into left field, Jonathan moved up to second, and Sterling had a chance to bring him in.

"What were you talking to Jonathan about?" Harlan asked Lian.

"I watched the catcher's signals. I figured them out. I told Jonathan I would touch my helmet if it was a change-up, and my shoulder if it was a curve."

Billy was listening in. He said, "Lian, you're *always* thinking."

Just then Sterling hit a fly ball to left. Easy out.

Now the Dodgers had to play *serious* defense.

They had a three-run lead, and the championship was just half an inning away!

Nugent was leading off. He was a tough guy to strike out, and he was very fast.

And he proved it.

He hit the ball on the ground toward left field. Jonathan made the stop deep in the hole. He threw hard, too, but he couldn't quite get Nugent.

So the Giants had a man on.

Harlan had hoped they could get out of the inning easier than that, but he also remembered what the coach had said. It was the team that kept its head and played smart that would win.

Harlan crouched behind the plate and signaled for a fastball, and Kenny hummed one. Cooper, the second baseman, took a good swing . . . and missed.

Harlan signaled fastball again and set the

target outside. Kenny came in with a hard one, just off the outside corner.

But Cooper chased it for strike two.

Then Harlan had Kenny waste a fastball a little inside, to set up for the curve.

The curve broke, and Cooper was leaning away when the umpire barked, *"STRIKE THREE!!!"*

"All right," Harlan came up yelling. "One away."

The Dodgers' infielders all held up one finger, and the outfield signaled back. No one wanted to forget how many outs there were at a time like this.

Weight was coming up. He could knock the ball out of California and the Dodgers would still have the lead. But Harlan didn't want things to get that close.

He thought it might be smart to mix things up and start Weight with a curve. It was a good idea, but Weight's instincts were too good. He drove the pitch to right field for a single.

Nugent used his speed to motor around second and head for third. Anthony made a bluff as though he might throw to third, but he used his head and ran toward the infield, and then flipped the ball in to Jonathan.

But Glenn was coming up, and he could score the tying run. No way did Harlan want to see this guy get on base. He was also a guy who could hit a home run.

Harlan signaled fastball, and Kenny rifled one in at the knees. Glenn got a bat on it and fouled it off.

Then hard and inside, and Glenn let the pitch go by.

"Steee-rike."

It had been close, and Harlan wasn't expecting the call.

Neither was Glenn. He was mad.

Harlan wanted a curve now, but Kenny shook him off and stayed with the fastball. He fired a beauty, but Glenn timed it.

He hit it on the nose.

The ball skimmed across the infield grass on a couple of hops, heading for right field.

Harlan cringed. He was sure a run would score.

But Lian flashed toward the ball. He dove, made the stop, leaped up, and fired to second.

Jonathan had seen the play coming and

he made his move right on time. He took the throw as he strode over the bag, dragged his right foot across the base, and kept his eye on first.

"Oooouuut!"

Jonathan was still in motion. He fired a perfect strike to Jenny at first.

"Oooooo-uuuuut!!"

Double play!

Double play!!

It was all over.

DOUBLE PLAY!!!

The Dodgers had taken it all.

The whole team charged toward the infield. They bounced and jumped and screamed, and then they all crash-landed on the mound in a huge pileup.

"We're going to the *district tournament!*" Billy screamed. "No one's going to stop us now!"

And everyone cheered in response.

As they rolled off the pile everyone began to grab each other and shout their congratulations. But it was Jonathan who bellowed, "Lian's the hero! He did *everything* today!"

And suddenly everyone was mobbing Lian and then hoisting him upon their shoulders.

He kept saying, "No, please. Let me down. I didn't do so much."

But no one believed him.

They carried him over to the coach, who was still standing near third base, grinning wide, enjoying every minute of this.

The players finally set Lian down, and he looked way up at the coach and smiled.

"I told you we had to play smart," Coach Wilkens said. "But Lian was more than smart. He was *brilliant!*"

Lian only said, "Thank you, Coach" and nodded his head.

By then parents were streaming out on the field. Harlan spotted Lian's parents, smiling but waiting politely for a chance to congratulate their son.

When Lian saw them, he ran to them, and they both grabbed him in their arms at the same time.

Just as Harlan was about to head for his own parents, Mr. Jie stopped him.

"You were very kind to Lian. We thank

you," he said. He reached out to shake Harlan's hand.

But Lian stepped up and said, "No, Dad, we do this." He turned toward Harlan, then leaped up and slapped his hand.

Mr. Jie grinned and then gave Harlan a polite high-five of his own and one to Lian.

And then the other players began to come over, and Mr. Jie—and even Mrs. Jie—high-fived them all.

Lian laughed and laughed. And he kept yelling to all his friends on the team, "We're champs! We're champs!"

Championship Play-off
BOX SCORE, GAME 21

Blue Springs Giants 0   Angel Park Dodgers 3

	ab	r	h	rbi		ab	r	h	rbi
Nugent lf	2	0	1	0	Jie 2b	3	2	2	0
Cooper 2b	3	0	0	0	White 3b	2	1	1	0
Weight 3b	2	0	2	0	Sandoval p	2	0	1	2
Glenn p	3	0	0	0	Swingle ss	3	0	1	1
Sanchez ss	2	0	0	0	Roper 1b	2	0	1	0
Spinner cf	1	0	0	0	Malone cf	3	0	0	0
Dodero c	1	0	0	0	Scott rf	0	0	0	0
Hausberg 1b	2	0	1	0	Bacon c	1	0	0	0
Waganheim rf	1	0	0	0	Boschi lf	1	0	0	0
Zonn cf	1	0	0	0	Ruiz rf	1	0	0	0
Villareal c	1	0	0	0	Sloan c	1	0	0	0
Stevens rf	1	0	0	0	Riddle lf	1	0	0	0
ttl	**20**	**0**	**4**	**0**		**20**	**3**	**6**	**3**

Giants   0 0 0   0 0 0—0
Dodgers   2 0 0   0 1 x—3

Second Season

League Standings After Ten Games:
(Second Half of Season)

Dodgers	9–1	Padres	4–6
Giants	8–2	Mariners	3–7
Reds	5–5	A's	1–9

Sixth Game Scores:

Dodgers	9	Mariners	8
Giants	7	Padres	6
Reds	15	A's	7

Seventh Game Scores:

Dodgers	4	Reds	0
Giants	6	Mariners	2
A's	14	Padres	13

Eighth Game Scores:

Dodgers	14	A's	2
Giants	3	Reds	2
Padres	7	Mariners	4

Ninth Game Scores:

Dodgers	8	Padres	6
Giants	16	A's	0
Mariners	5	Reds	4

Tenth Game Scores:

Dodgers	4	Giants	1
Padres	6	Reds	0
Mariners	17	A's	3

Championship Play-off

Dodgers	3	Giants	0

JONATHAN SWINGLE

At-bats	Runs	Hits	RBIs	Avg.
63	30	42	39	.667

SECOND-YEAR STATISTICS

JENNY ROPER

At-bats	Runs	Hits	RBIs	Avg.
45	13	25	19	.556

KENNY SANDOVAL

At-bats	Runs	Hits	RBIs	Avg.
71	27	37	26	.521

SECOND-YEAR STATISTICS

JACOB SCOTT

At-bats	Runs	Hits	RBIs	Avg.
51	13	25	15	.490

SECOND-YEAR STATISTICS

LIAN JIE

At-bats	Runs	Hits	RBIs	Avg.
61	16	28	10	.459

STERLING MALONE

At-bats	Runs	Hits	RBIs	Avg.
63	12	27	22	.429

SECOND-YEAR STATISTICS

HENRY WHITE

At-bats	Runs	Hits	RBIs	Avg.
73	22	29	7	.397

SECOND-YEAR STATISTICS

HARLAN SLOAN

At-bats	Runs	Hits	RBIs	Avg.
32	8	11	5	.344

BILLY BACON

At-bats	Runs	Hits	RBIs	Avg.
29	7	8	5	.276

SECOND-YEAR STATISTICS

EDDIE BOSCHI

At-bats	Runs	Hits	RBIs	Avg.
50	7	9	1	.180

SECOND-YEAR STATISTICS

BEN RIDDLE

At-bats	Runs	Hits	RBIs	Avg.
28	3	5	3	.179

ANTHONY RUIZ

At-bats	Runs	Hits	RBIs	Avg.
23	0	3	0	.130

ALL-STAR OF THE MONTH

JONATHAN SWINGLE

Jonathan is one of those rare athletes who "has it all." He has quick reactions, great speed, power, and coordination. He's a "natural." But where much is given, much is expected. And sometimes Jonathan has had trouble handling all those expectations.

Jonathan came to the Dodgers after moving to Angel Park from Los Angeles. He was a star on a big city team—the best hitter *and* the best pitcher—and he certainly has been the star of the Dodgers. He has hit for average (how about .733 for the first half?!), and he has led the team in home runs and in runs batted in. In addition, he has been the pitching star for the team all year. If the Dodgers are a team of stars, then Jonathan has to be called a *super*star!

But Jonathan is not always the steady, solid player he would like to be, and he knows it. He sometimes lets little things get under his skin, and then he loses some of his control. Opposing players like to needle Jonathan because they know they can get to him. And once they do, Jonathan has trouble getting strikes over the plate or keeping his concentration when he's up to bat. Or at least, that's how things have been. Jonathan knows he has to work on keeping his control, and he has improved a great deal.

Those who know Jonathan best know that he has some special challenges to deal with. Maybe he's blessed with great talent, but life hasn't always been easy for him in other ways. Jonathan's father is a construction worker who suffered a serious injury to his back when Jonathan was in third grade. Since then, he has been in and out of hospitals a number of times, and he has often been out of work. The financial pressure has not been easy, and Jonathan's family life has been rocky at times.

Mr. Swingle wants his son to succeed, as all parents do, but sometimes he puts too much pressure on Jonathan. Jonathan often feels that he has to be perfect to satisfy his father. Mr. Swingle wants him to pitch no-hitters and strike out everyone all the time, it seems, but no one can do that. What Jonathan feels much of the time is the fear that he will let his father down. And yet Jonathan would never admit that. Unfortunately, Jonathan has a tendency to cover up his fears with a cocky style. And it's just that style that sometimes gets him in trouble.

Still, Jonathan is an amazing athlete. He not only is a fine basketball player, he's a flash as a sprinter, too. He's destined to shine at any sport he plays. But he needs to make sure he does just as well in school. Then again, that's another problem he's made progress on. His fifth-grade teacher recently told his parents that he'd suddenly caught hold and is doing better than ever. Maybe Jonathan is growing up a little. He has the talent, and he knows what it's going to take to make him a complete person in all areas of his life. Some kids wait too long to get that all figured out. Jonathan appears to be getting himself straightened out just in time.